THE DAY SUN WAS STOLEN

JAMIE OLIVIERO

ILLUSTRATED BY

SHARON HITCHCOCK

HYPERION BOOKS FOR CHILDREN
NEW YORK

When the world was new, Raven created all the animals. He scooped up some clay and shaped it into a round body and fishtail and called it Seal. Then he did the same things again, only this time he jumped up and down on the tail to flatten it and called his creation Beaver.

Finally only one lump of clay remained. While he thought about what to create, Raven rolled the clay in the mud and moss—back and forth, back and forth. When the lump became large and round, Raven breathed life into it and made Bear.

Because Raven had rolled the clay back and forth, back and forth through the moss, Bear's coat was twice as thick and twice as furry as any other animal's. When Sun shone down, all the other animals welcomed the warmth, but not Bear. Sun's rays

bothered him and made him hot. Day after day Bear sweltered
in the heat. Finally, when he could stand it no longer, he reared
up, shook his huge furry paws at Sun, and said, "I'm going to
get you!"

Bear was determined to stop Sun from shining. He walked and walked until he came to the highest mountain. Then he climbed higher and higher until he reached its snowcapped peak. Sun watched as Bear scooped up some snow and put it

into his mouth. Then Bear reached up, yanked Sun out of the sky, and held him in his mouth. Bear's mouth was so cold from the snow that Sun couldn't burn it and Bear walked triumphantly back to his cave.

In front of the cave, Bear rolled aside a rock that was too
large and heavy for anyone else to move, uncovering a deep

hole. He placed Sun inside and pushed the rock back in place.
"That takes care of that," he said with a growl.

Without Sun the world was cold and gray. That didn't
bother Bear because his coat was so thick and furry, but all
the other animals began to shiver. When Raven saw how his

creatures were suffering, he began to cry. The world became
cold and gray and rainy.

The people who lived in the camp beside the river began to complain. They wanted Sun back. A young boy named Ts'ina dabju (cheena dabjoo), which means small fish, asked his wise grandmother what had made Sun disappear.

"It is Bear," she said. "Bear has stolen Sun."

The boy knew he had to help the animals and his people, but he was afraid of Bear. Finally, after many days, he thought of a plan.

"I will trick Bear into releasing Sun," the boy said to Grandmother. "When he goes to the river to eat, I will go there and put on the magic fish skin you keep in your medicine pouch and hide until Bear has eaten three fish.

Bear always eats three fish. Once he has finished eating, I will dive into the water and let him catch me. By that time he will be so full he will take me to his cave and save me for later. When he is asleep, I will fix him so that he will want to let Sun go."

Grandmother was proud of Ts'ina dabju's bravery. She watched him go to the river's edge, and when he began to pull the fish skin over his feet, she returned to camp. As Ts'ina dabju pulled,

the fish skin began to stretch until it covered his body. He
looked just like a fish. When he saw Bear catch his third fish,
Ts'ina dabju splashed into the water.

Everything happened as planned. Bear caught the boy in the fish skin but was too full to eat him. He carried his prize catch

back to the cave, dropped him in a corner, and settled down
for a nap.

As soon as Bear was sleeping, Ts'ina dabju jumped up,
peeled off the fish skin, and took out of his pocket a clamshell

that Grandmother had given him. He sharpened the shell on a stone and began to shave the sleeping bear.

Soon the boy had shaved off so much fur that Bear's coat
was only half as thick as it had been. The boy scooped up the

shaved fur and stuffed it into a sack to carry away so Bear could not stick it back on.

Holding the sack in one hand and stuffing the rolled-up fish skin in his pocket, the boy tiptoed out of the cave. As he ran back to the camp through the forest, a branch tore a hole in the sack and all of Bear's fur was scattered by the wind.

Ts'ina dabju returned to camp and gave Grandmother the fish skin to put in her medicine pouch. "Let us now see what happens," he said.

When Bear woke up, he was surprised to feel his body shivering and his teeth chattering. He had never been cold before and for the first time he desired the warmth of Sun.

Bear ran to the rock, rolled it aside, grabbed Sun, and tossed him so high that he stuck in the sky. Soon Sun—who had lost most of his heat in the hole—regained his brilliance, and all the animals of the forest and the people of the camp were warm again. Raven was pleased and no longer cried for his creatures.

Bear liked his thinner coat. It was more comfortable.
However, when winter came he began to shiver. With his new

coat he could not stand the cold. When North Wind began to blow, Bear refused to go outside and decided to sleep.

But some of the other animals had gathered Bear's scattered fur and saved it. When the weather grew colder they added it to their own coats. And that is why, to this day, some woodland

animals grow thicker fur in the winter to keep themselves warm, while Bear sleeps.

The Haida live on the Queen Charlotte Islands near British Columbia, Canada, as well as the islands off the coast of Washington State and southeastern and northern Alaska. Although today they live more settled lives, for centuries they lived in camps and migrated for seasonal hunting and fishing. Their houses, made from red cedar planks hewn from standing trees, were built close together and faced the beach. Transportation was mainly by canoe. The prosperity of the tribe, the importance of family, and the traditions of ceremony and carving were and continue to be central to their culture.

The Haida believe that in ancient times there were no distinctions between humans, animals, and spirits. Each could take on the form of the other by either changing shape or putting on the skin of an animal (such as the fish skin in this tale). Although that time is now lost, the ability is remembered through Haida art, dance, and song. Common Haida folklore tells how that world changed into this one and recounts the adventures of Raven and Eagle, the heads of the two social clans within the tribe.

Raven and Eagle are central characters depicted on totem poles. The figures are typically highly stylized flat designs hand-carved onto a curved surface. Principal colors are black, red, and blue green. In this book Haida artist Sharon Hitchcock's paintings draw upon these rich artistic traditions.

For more information address Hyperion Books for Children,
114 Fifth Avenue, New York, New York 10011.

FIRST EDITION
1   3   5   7   9   10   8   6   4   2
Designed by A.O.Osen

Library of Congress Cataloging-in-Publication Data
Oliviero, Jamie
The day Sun was stolen/Jamie Oliviero;
illustrated by Sharon Hitchcock—1st ed.
p.   cm.
ISBN 0-7868-0031-3 (trade)—ISBN 0-7868-2026-8 (lib. bdg.)
1. Haida Indians—Folklore.   I. Hitchcock, Sharon, ill.   II. Title.
E99.H2045   1995   94–19374
398.22'089972—dc20

The illustrations are prepared using gouache and acrylics.
This book is set in 14-point Palatino.

Endsheets: The two-character totem pole depicts Raven (top) and Bear (beneath). The one-character pole has a ringed column atop the figure of Bear. The use of Bear in this column tells the viewer that this symbolic animal is an important element in that clan's family history. The column's rings symbolize the number of elaborate ceremonial feasts, or potlatches, that have been held by that particular clan. Totem poles were typically placed in front of family homes or surrounding community meeting places.

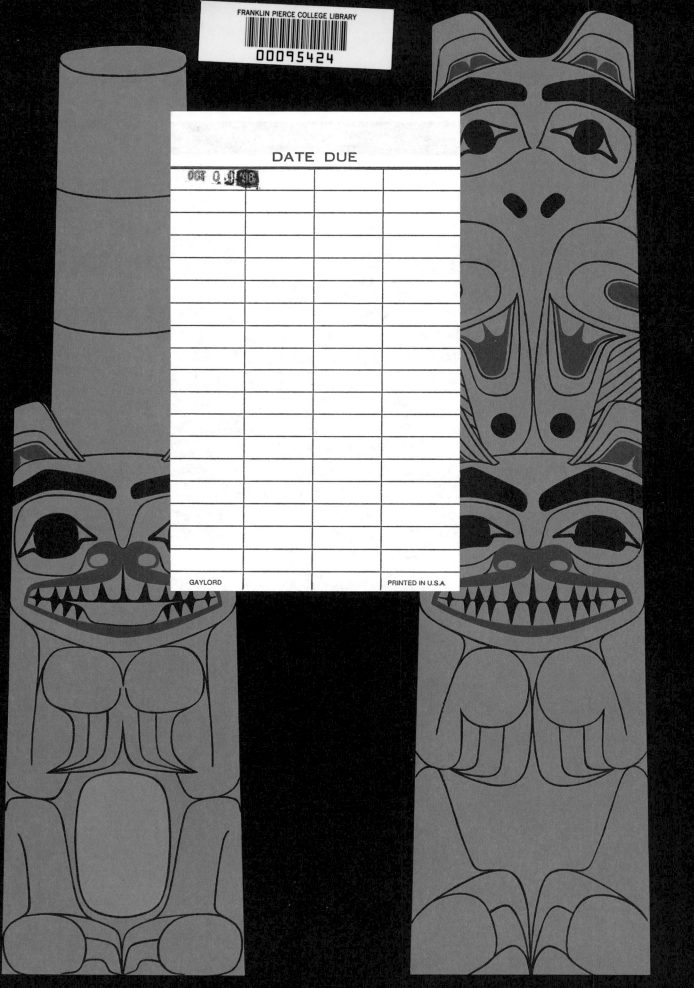